Slobcat is our cat.
He does nothing but
lie about and sleep.

PAUL GERAGHTY

SLOBCAT

Mini Treasures

RED FOX

1 3 5 7 9 10 8 6 4 2

Text and illustrations © 1991 Paul Geraghty

Paul Geraghty has asserted his right under the Copyright,
Designs and Patents Act, 1988
to be identified as author and illustrator of this work

First published in the United Kingdom 1991
by Hutchinson Children's Books
First published in Mini Treasures edition 1996
by Red Fox
Random House, 20 Vauxhall Bridge Road, London SW1V 2SA

Random House Australia (Pty) Limited
20 Alfred Street, Milsons Point, Sydney,
New South Wales 2061, Australia

Random House New Zealand Limited
18 Poland Road, Glenfield,
Auckland 10, New Zealand

Random House South Africa (Pty) Limited
PO Box 2263, Rosebank 2121, South Africa

Random House UK Limited Reg. No. 954009

A CIP catalogue record for this book
is available from the British Library

ISBN 009 9725 711

Printed in Singapore

Heaven knows what
he does when we're
not there.

But when we get home he's still sleeping. That's why we call him Slobcat.

When it's his dinner time,
he's nowhere to be seen ...

... and when we do find him,
he's even too lazy to eat.

I don't know *where* he goes
when we put him out ...

... but he often comes back soaking wet because he's too lazy to shelter from the rain.

He spends so much
time inside ...

... that he ends up getting in the way!

Last week Mum saw a
mouse, so Dad put
out a trap ...

... because Slobcat
isn't interested
in chasing mice.

All *he's* interested in is lying about in the sun.

Luckily,
we don't have rats ...

... because if we did,
Dad says we'd have to
get a proper cat.

Some people have
dangerous animals
in their gardens.

But for some reason
they don't come
into ours.

It's strange because
the little creatures
don't seem afraid.

Sometimes, when we're asleep, there are burglars about.

Thank goodness
we have Brutus to
frighten them
off ...

... because Slobcat couldn't frighten a flea!

People say that all cats have a secret
life that we don't know about ...

... but I'm sure Slobcat's
much too lazy for that!